Creator of the Mr Men and
the John Mouse series

Published by Hodder & Stoughton

Count Worm
Albert the alphabetical elephant
Hippo · Potto · Mouse Books

ISBN 0 340 21500 3

Copyright © 1977 Roger Hargreaves
First published in 1977
Printed and bound in Great Britain, for Hodder & Stoughton Children's Books,
a division of Hodder & Stoughton Ltd, Arlen House, Salisbury Road, Leicester,
by Cox & Wyman Ltd, London, Fakenham and Reading

GRANDFATHER CLOCK

Story and pictures by

Roger Hargreaves

HODDER & STOUGHTON

Grandfather Clock lives in
Ticktock Cottage.

He's a nice old chap, and everybody likes him. Particularly because of one thing he can do which nobody else can do.

He can tell you the time!
Now, that doesn't sound like something nobody else can do.
Does it?

But Grandfather Clock doesn't tell you the time
like other people tell you the time.
Oh no. He turns into the time.

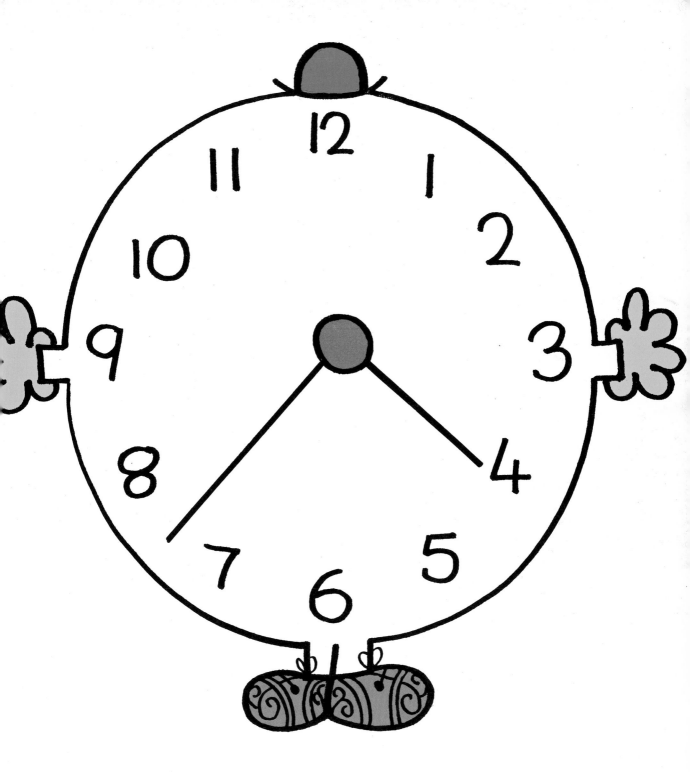

Just like that!

Early one morning Grandfather Clock was fast asleep in his
bedroom at Ticktock Cottage.
A bird started singing outside his bedroom window.
And that woke him up.
"Oh," he yawned, "I wonder what time it is?"

And he turned himself into the time and looked at himself.
The big hand pointed to his number 12.
The little hand pointed to his number 5.
"Oh no," he groaned. "It's only 5 o'clock, and that's much
too early to get up." So, he turned himself back into himself.
And turned over and went back to sleep.

Later he awoke again.
This time the big hand pointed to his top.
And the little hand pointed to number 7.
"That's better," he said, "7 o'clock. And that's getting-up time." So he got up.

Grandfather Clock had a boiled egg for breakfast.
Boiled for exactly 4 minutes.
It's quite useful being a clock as well as a person!

And after breakfast he went for a walk.
He met Farmer Smiles on his way to market.
"Can you tell me the time please?" smiled Farmer Smiles.
"Certainly," replied Grandfather Clock.

His big hand pointed to his top.
And his little hand pointed to his number 9.
"Oh dear," said Farmer Smiles, not smiling.
"It's 9 o'clock. I'm late for market."

And off he rushed.

He walked until the little hand had moved from number 9 to number 12. Both hands were pointing to his number 12.

"Hello," said old Mrs Chuckle who was looking over the
garden hedge. "It's 12 o'clock."
"That's lunchtime," said Grandfather Clock.
"That's right," chuckled Mrs Chuckle, and invited him
in for lunch.

That afternoon Grandfather Clock continued his walk. He was passing a school when the teacher put his head out of a window. "I know what you're going to ask me," grinned Grandfather Clock, and he turned himself into the time.

The big hand pointed to his top.
And the little hand pointed to his number 4.
"4 o'clock," said the teacher.
"Hometime," shouted all the children in his class.
Grandfather Clock walked along with two of the children
from the school.

"The big hand's pointing to your top," cried the boy.

"And your little hand's pointing to 7," cried the girl.

"And that means it's 7 o'clock," said Grandfather Clock.

"And that means it's bathtime," said the children's mother.

"Come along."

"Is it true you can turn yourself into the time?" they asked.
"Definitely," he smiled.
"Will you come home with us and show us?" they asked.
"Certainly," he laughed.
   Later, he showed them how he could turn into the time.

After their bath the children put on their pyjamas, and Grandfather Clock read them a story.
"What time is it now?" they asked when he had finished.
Grandfather Clock showed them.

"The big hand's pointing to your top," said the girl.
"But your little hand's moved on to your number 8," said the boy.
"So the time is 8 o'clock," said Grandfather Clock.
"So it's bedtime," said the children's mother.

The children went to bed.
And Grandfather Clock went home.

By the time he arrived back at Ticktock Cottage
the big hand was pointing to his top, and the little hand
was pointing to his number 10.
10 o'clock! And that's late!

It was
so late,
and he was so
tired after walking all day,
he went straight to bed. In fact, he was so tired,
do you know how long Grandfather Clock slept for?

Right round the clock!